In memory of my grandfather, Samuel Kernish
—C.B.

Text copyright © 1994 by Cynthia Benjamin.
Illustrations copyright © 1994 by Jacqueline Rogers.
All rights reserved. Published by Scholastic Inc.
Printed in the U.S.A.

ISBN 0-439-45161-2

2 3 4 5 6 7 8 9 10   23   11 10 09 08 07 06 05 04 03

Footprints
in the Snow

by Cynthia Benjamin
Illustrated by Jacqueline Rogers

SCHOLASTIC INC.

New York   Toronto   London   Auckland   Sydney
Mexico City   New Delhi   Hong Kong   Buenos Aires

Winter snow falls.

Winter wind blows.

Someone hops

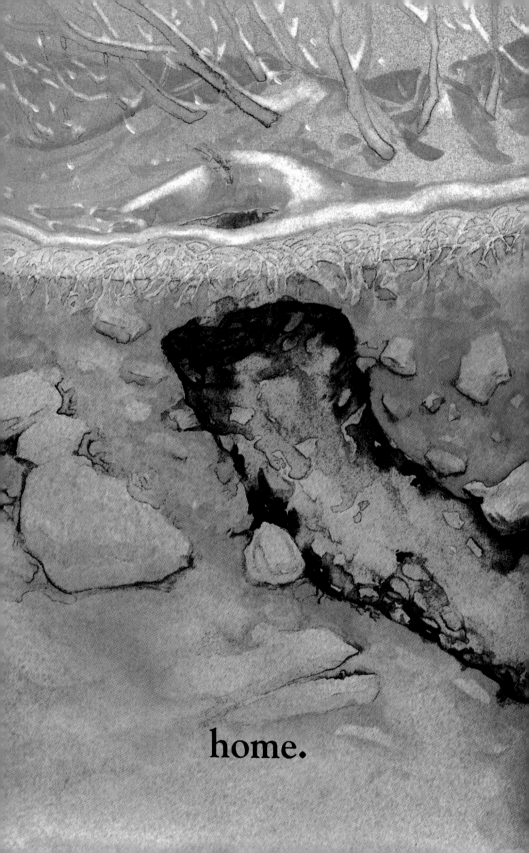

home.

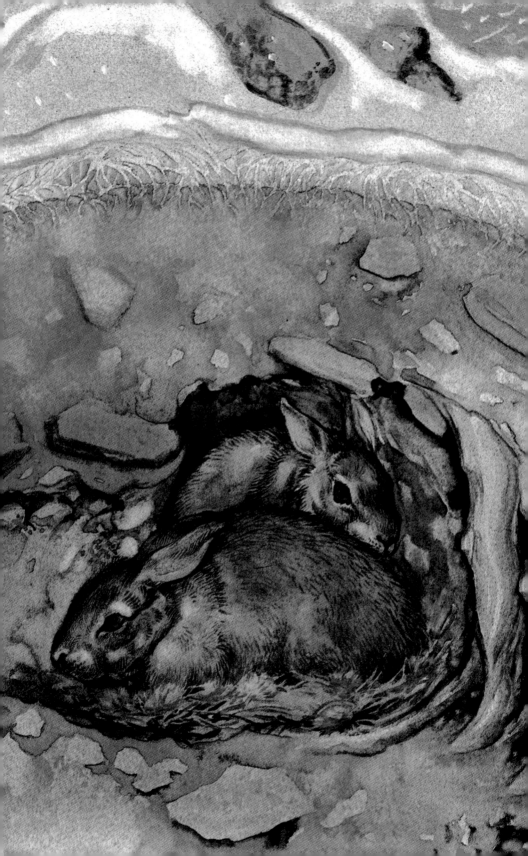

Someone runs

home.

Someone stomps

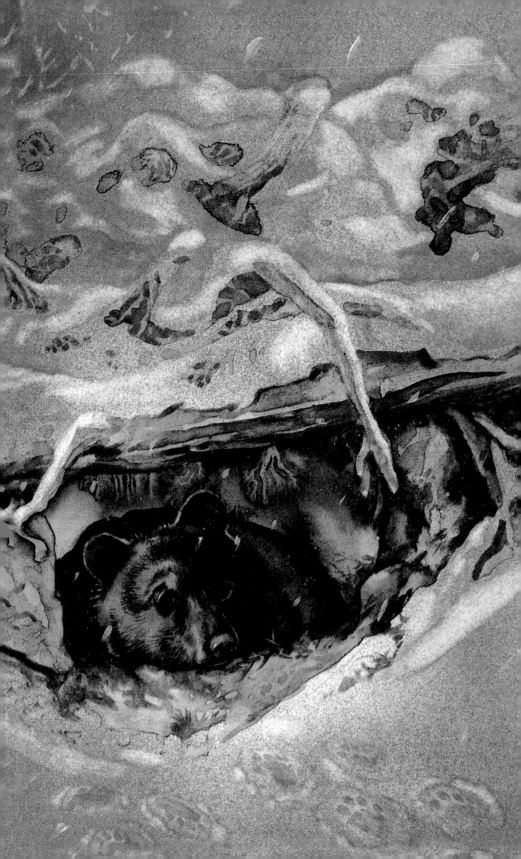

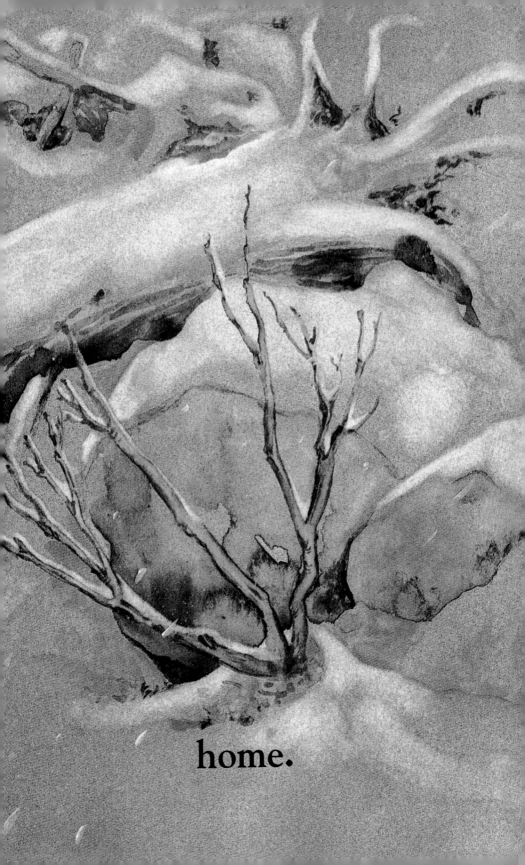

home.

Someone swims

home.

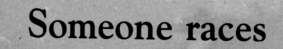

Someone races

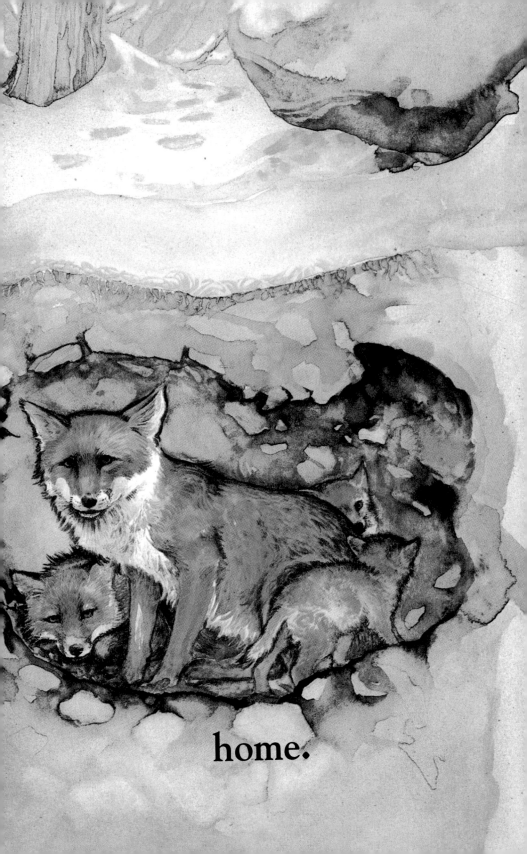

home.

Someone flies

home.

Someone hurries

home.

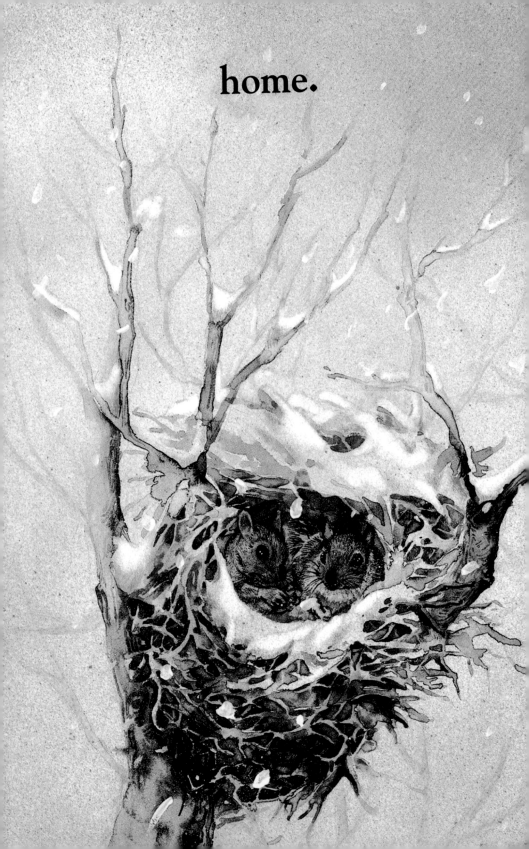

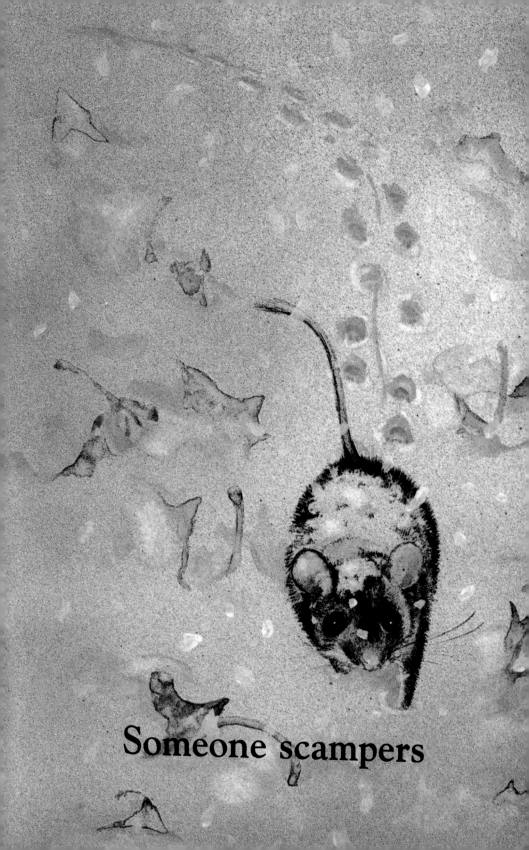

Someone scampers

home.

Someone walks

home.

Winter snow falls.
Winter wind blows.